Contents

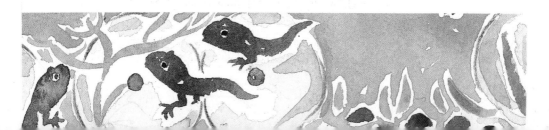

The Tickle Rhyme

"Who's that tickling my back?" said the wall.

"Me," said a small

caterpillar. "I'm learning

to crawl."

Ian Serraillier

Little Joe

Did you ever hear about Sal and Tom's
baby brother? His name was Joe. They called him
little Joe. And little Joe was always into big trouble.

One day his dad was doing the washing. Tom was
helping. Joe was not helping. He was not helping at all.

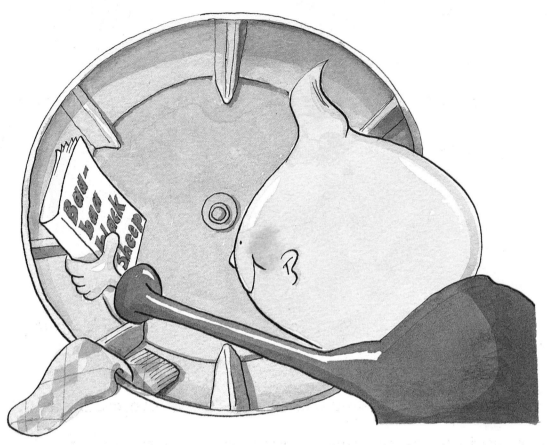

"Here's a book," said Sal. "Why don't you look at the book, Joe."

"Book!" said Joe, and he smiled a big smile. (Oh Oh!) But do you think he looked at the book? Oh no. Not little Joe.

As soon as no one was looking at him, he put the book in the washing machine.

Then his dad put in some more washing. He shut the door and put the machine on.

Round and round went the book in the machine, round and round until it was so wet it fell to bits. Then the machine stopped. It wouldn't go.

And all because of little Joe.

That was big trouble.

It took Dad and Sal and Tom a long time to fix the washing machine.

"All gone book," said Joe.

After that, they went out to do the shopping.

On the way home Dad took out the keys for the

door. Joe saw them.

"Key!" said Joe. "Key key key key!"

He shouted and shouted.

"I think he wants to play with the keys, Dad,"

said Sal.

"I know. I know! And all right, Joe," said Dad.

"Just stop that noise. Now here are the keys.

You can play with them but do look after them."

"Key!" said Joe, and he smiled a big smile.
(Oh Oh!) Well, do you think he looked after the
keys? Oh no. Not little Joe.

As soon as no one was looking at him, he put the
keys in the dustbin! So now how were they going to
get in?

Dad put the shopping down by the door.

"Can we have the keys please, Joe?" he said.

Joe smiled.

"Oh no!" said Sal and Tom. "Where are the keys, Joe?"

But all Joe said was, "Keys. All gone."

They looked and looked. They looked everywhere but they couldn't find the keys. So they had to go all the way to their friends in the next street to get some other keys.

By the time they got into the house again they were all very tired and hungry. Little Joe was very, very tired.

"Here's a sandwich, Joe," said Dad. "You go and eat the sandwich while we make the tea."

"Mmm," said Joe, and he smiled a tired smile. (Oh Oh!) But did he eat the sandwich, do you think? Oh no. Not little Joe.

As soon as no one was looking at him, he went and put the sandwich in the video machine!

And that was big trouble. Big BIG trouble!

But by the time the others found out, little Joe was fast asleep.

No trouble at all.

After a bath

After my bath
I try, try, try
to wipe myself
till I'm dry, dry, dry.

Hands to wipe
and fingers and toes
and two wet legs
and a shiny nose.

Just think how much
less time I'd take
if I were a dog
and could shake, shake, shake.

Aileen Fisher

One fine day

One fine day in the middle of the night

Two dead men got up to fight;

Back to back they faced each other,

Drew their swords and shot each other.

Traditional

Grow up, Doodle!

"When I grow up," said Doodle, "I shall be a
grasshopper."

"A grasshopper?" said his mother. "You won't.
You'll be a frog. Like me. Like all of us. Like your
brothers."

"But why?" said Doodle. "Why not a grasshopper?
Just think of it. I could jump and hop in the long grass –"

"You can jump and hop when you are a frog," said
his mother. "Now swim along and have your tea."

Doodle came back again at once.

"I know!" he said. "I'll be a bird! Just think of it! I could fly from tree to tree –"

"If you try to fly from tree to tree," said his mother, "you'll come down to earth in no time. Frogs jump and hop; they don't fly. Now, go and sleep."

But as Doodle tried to sleep, he thought of all the other things that he could be. A rabbit? He could hop all over the park. A squirrel? That would be fun, up in the trees.

"I'm tired of being just a small tadpole," he thought.

All tadpoles are small, and Doodle was very, very small. All his brothers were very big tadpoles. When their mother called them, they always got there first. When Doodle came up, they let him eat what they didn't want. He was small and unhappy and always hungry.

"When I grow up I shall be something big, like an elephant," he said.

"You'll be a frog," said his mother. "You'll be a frog — and like it!"

"You'll be a frog — and like it!" said his brothers.
"But just a little one. Not like us." And off they
went to find more to eat. They were always eating
now, and were very, very big. As time went by, they
got very big-headed about it.

Doodle looked at them.

"All head and no tail," he thought. "I can't help
being small."

Then he noticed something. His big-headed
brothers had got legs! Little baby legs!

"It's not fair!" he shouted. "I'm the one who wants to do something exciting. I'm the one who wants to be a grasshopper. Or a rabbit. Or a squirrel. It's not fair!"

His brothers smiled all over their big heads, and went on eating. They waved their little baby legs and looked for more to eat.

Doodle went off on his own. He would forget all about his big-headed brothers. He would grow up how he liked – on his own.

For the first time ever, he could eat all he wanted.
His mother came to see him and noticed him get as
fat and as big-headed as his brothers.

"You'll be a frog any day now," she said. "You'll
be a frog – and like it!" But Doodle shook his big head
and waved his new little legs.

"I'm going to be a grasshopper," he said.

He never noticed his brothers jump out of the
water. He never noticed that they now looked just
like their mother. He just noticed that his back legs
had started to grow and that his tail had gone
small.

"With legs like these, I'll be a grasshopper in no
time," he thought, and he waited to see what would
grow next.

But there was nothing more. Perhaps he was a
squirrel after all? No – not with this little baby tail.
A rabbit, then? Well, no, not a rabbit.

He jumped up out of the river. The grass and the
cold wet mud all around him were lovely. With one
long hop, he set off to find his brothers.

He was a frog – and he liked it!

A baby sardine

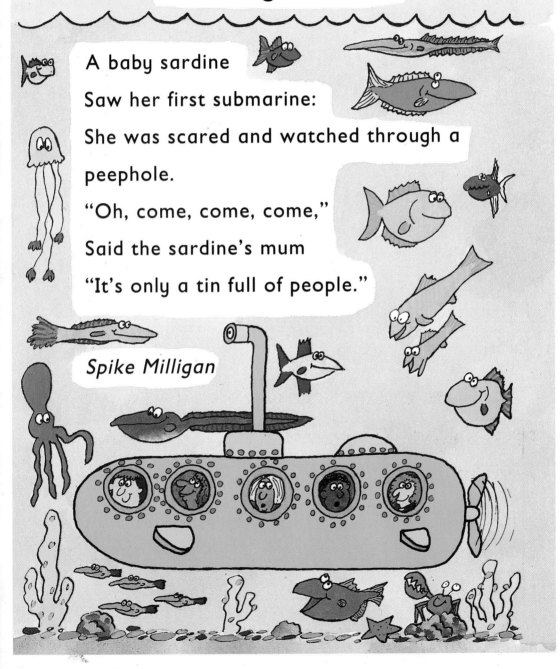

A baby sardine

Saw her first submarine:

She was scared and watched through a

peephole.

"Oh, come, come, come,"

Said the sardine's mum

"It's only a tin full of people."

Spike Milligan

Diplodocus

When Diplodocus gives a smile
It makes his eyes go crinkly.
He stays in water all day long
That's why his skin is wrinkly.

Margaret Ryan

The very proud elephant

Elephant took some bananas with his long grey trunk. Elephant was very fond of bananas. He was also very proud of his long grey trunk.

"It is the best trunk in the jungle," he said. "We should have a competition to see who has the best trunk. I am sure I would win."

"That's not fair," said Rhinoceros, who was near by. "I don't have a trunk, but I do have a horn. I am very proud of my horn."

"Well, then," said Elephant. "We should have a best trunk and a best horn competition. I am sure we would win."

"What about me?" said Parrot, who was flying by. "I don't have a trunk. I don't have a horn but I do have some very fine feathers. I am very proud of my feathers."

"Well, then," said Elephant. "We should have a best trunk and a best horn and a best feathers competition. I am sure we would win."

"What about me?" said Crocodile, who was in the river. "I don't have a trunk. I don't have a horn. I don't have any feathers but I do have some fine big teeth. I am very proud of my teeth."

"Well, then," said Elephant. "We should have a best trunk and a best horn and a best feathers and a best teeth competition. I am sure we would win."

"What about me?" said Monkey, who was in a
tree. "I don't have a trunk. I don't have a horn.
I don't have any feathers. I don't have very big teeth
but I do have a long curly tail. I am very proud of
my curly tail."

"Well, then, we should have a best trunk and a
best horn and a best feathers and a best teeth and
a best curly tail competition," said Elephant. "I am
sure we would win."

So they did have a competition. They walked
round and round to see who would win.

Well, you can guess who won the prize for the
best trunk.

Elephant!

And you can guess who won the prize for the
best horn.

Rhinoceros!

And you can guess who won the prize for the best feathers.

Parrot!

And you can guess who won the prize for the best teeth.

Crocodile!

And you can guess who won the prize for the best curly tail.

Monkey!

But can you guess what the prizes were?

Lots of bananas! Elephant started to hand them out.

"I don't like bananas," said Rhinoceros. "I will have some fresh green leaves for a prize."

"I don't like bananas either," said Parrot. "I will have a very big nut for a prize."

"And I don't like bananas either," said Crocodile. "I will have a big fish for a prize."

"I do like bananas," said Monkey. 'But I like mangoes even better. I will have a mango for a prize."

Elephant was very happy. He had the best trunk in the jungle and had won lots of bananas!